the Alphabet set
by
Matt Lumby
Published by Matt Lumby Books
www.mattlumbybooks.com
I0714422

"Oh dear me!"
sighed Elemenno Pee
As he wandered on to
the page you see.

"I'm all mixed up
and I just don't know
Who I am
and where I need to go!"

Suddenly out of nowhere fell
Aitch-Eye Jaykay, lost as well.

"Who is this?"
said Elemenno Pee.
"Don't I know you?
Let me see..."

Then out of the blue
with a cry of "Yes!"
Came a very excited Cue-Arr Ess.

"He's your neighbour,
just like me!"
Said Cue-Arr Ess to Elemenno Pee.

Tee-Yoo Vee then arrived on her own
and softly cried "I'm all alone!"

"Don't you worry, just stick with me"
Said Cue-Arr Ess to Tee-Yoo Vee.

Next came Ay-Bee Seedy too
Who said to everyone,
"I'll help you!
Stand behind me, you'll be fine"
And he marched right up to
the front of the line.

But Ay-Bee Seedy looked quite cross
When Double-Yoo Ex yelled,
"I'll be the boss!"

(And sneaking along
so no one could hear,
Ee-Eff Gee said
"I'll just stand here")

Now the letters were really jumbled.
"This is all wrong!"
They griped and grumbled.

Then came a voice
that calmly said,
"I think I can help you.
I'm Wise Ed!"

"Ay-Bee Seedy starts this time,
Ee-Eff Gee is next in line,
Aitch-Eye Jaykay we can see
You belong with Elemenno Pee.

As for the rest, Cue-Arr Ess
You should be with Tee-Yoo Vee,
Double-Yoo Ex goes here instead,
And right at the end it's me, Wise Ed.

Now we've sorted out this mess
Let's all try to look our best!"

So they all linked up
And they held very tight
And they pulled very hard
Till they all looked right.

Now we know we can't go wrong
When we sing The Alphabet Song...

''Ay-Bee Seedy, Ee-Eff Gee, Aitch-Eye Jaykay, Elemenno Pee

ABcDEfghijKlmn

Cue-Arr Ess, Tee-Yoo Vee, Double-Yoo Ex, Wise Ed…

opQRstuVWXYZ

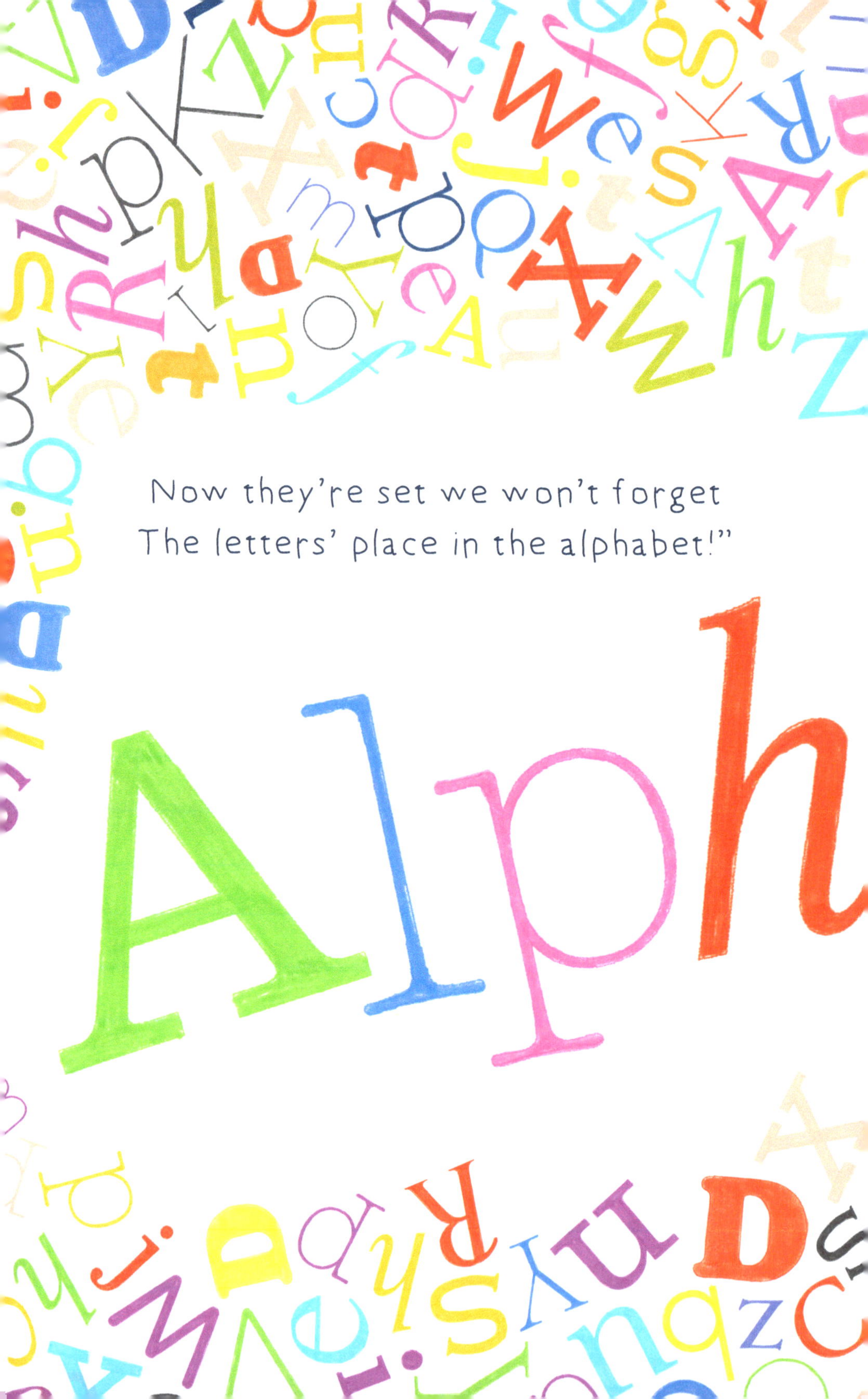

Now they're set we won't forget
The letters' place in the alphabet!"

Alph

the
Abet
set

Buy a copy of this book for your friends!

www.mattlumbybooks.com

9 780099 328290